Pony-Crazed Princess

Princess Ellie's Snowy Ride

Read all the adventures of Princess Ellie!

Pony-Crazed Princess

Princess Ellie's Snowy Ride

by Diana Kimpton

Illustrated by Lizzie Finlay

Hyperion Paperbacks for Children
New York

For Steve

First published in the United Kingdom in 2005 as
The Pony-Mad Princess: Princess Ellie's Holiday Adventure
by Usborne Publishing Ltd.
Based on an original concept by Anne Finnis
Text copyright © 2005 by Diana Kimpton and Anne Finnis
Illustrations copyright © 2005 by Lizzie Finlay

Printed in the United States of America
First U.S. edition, 2007
1 3 5 7 9 10 8 6 4 2

This book is set in 14.5-point Nadine Normal.

ISBN-13: 978-14231-0902-0
ISBN-10: 1-4231-0902-3

Visit www.hyperionbooksforchildren.com

Chapter 1

"Wow!" squealed Princess Ellie. "Look at those mountains."

"They're so huge," said her best friend, Kate. "And look, they've even got snow on the top."

"Of course they do," said Miss Stringle. "Andirovia is a much colder country than ours. Now stop pressing your face against the car window, Princess Aurelia. That's no way to behave. We can't have the public thinking princesses have squashed noses."

Ellie groaned as she sat back in her seat. She hated it when her governess called her by her real name. But she was too excited about going on a royal vacation to stay miserable for long. This was the first time she had ever visited her friend Prince John and his family. She had never been to Andirovia before. She gazed longingly at the white mountain peaks. "I've never seen real snow close up."

"I have," said Kate. "It's awesome. Mom and Dad took me skiing once." Kate's parents had to travel a lot for work, so she lived with her grandparents at the palace.

Her grandmother was the palace cook.

"Let's ask if we can go up there and make snowballs," suggested Ellie.

"You'll ask no such thing," declared Miss Stringle. "You are guests here, and you must go along with the activities your hosts have planned for you."

Ellie hoped some of those plans would involve Prince John's ponies. The country-side they were driving through looked perfect for riding. It was wild and free, with

meadows, forests, and fast-flowing mountain streams. Andirovia really was as wonderful as John had described.

The car slowed down. Ellie and Kate were traveling in the second car in a line of gleaming black vehicles, each of which had a small Andirovian flag fluttering at the front. Ellie's parents, the King and Queen, were in the first car. A few servants rode in the cars behind, along with the luggage. To Ellie's disappointment, there was no horse trailer. The King and Queen had insisted that all her ponies stay at home.

Ellie was already missing them. Just as she was thinking about grooming Moonbeam and Sundance, she caught sight of what had caused the cars to slow down. Up ahead a lady was riding a large, gray horse. The road was very narrow, so there wasn't room for the cars to pass the rider safely. They had to drive slowly behind her until she turned in to a gateway to let them get by.

As they swept past, Ellie gave the lady a royal wave, exactly as Miss Stringle had taught her. "What a beautiful horse," she sighed.

"Where?" asked Kate, who'd been staring out of the opposite window. She turned around just in time to catch a glimpse of the gray horse and its rider before the car sped past. Determined to see more, she swiveled around so she was kneeling on her seat. She watched them through the back window, waving wildly

at the rider with both hands.

"Sit down at once," snapped Miss Stringle. "That is not how the public expects royalty to behave."

"But I'm not royalty," said Kate.

Miss Stringle sighed. "I know that, and so do you. But that woman doesn't."

Kate turned around slowly and faced the front again. She slumped miserably in her seat. "I'm never going to get the hang of this," she groaned. "I just don't know how to act like royalty."

Ellie smiled reassuringly. "It's easy. If I can do it, anyone can."

"But you've had lots of practice," said Kate. "I haven't. I'm going to let everyone down. I know I am."

Ellie was desperate to cheer Kate up. She

knew her friend was nerv-
ous about coming along on
the royal vacation. But
Kate had every right to be
there. She had gotten her own
gold-edged invitation from the Emperor and
Empress of Andirovia. Prince John had
insisted on it.

It was Miss Stringle who came to Kate's
rescue. "Don't worry, my dear," she said
kindly. "Just follow Princess Aurelia. She
knows what to do."

Ellie stared at her in surprise. Her governess didn't usually express so much confi-
dence in her abilities.

At that moment, the cars turned a corner,
and Ellie saw Prince John's home for the
first time. "Wow!" she said for the second

time that day. John had been telling the truth.

His palace really was twice the size of the one she lived in. It was built of white stone, with huge towers located at each corner. It looked just like a castle.

"Look! There's a moat," cried Kate, "and swans."

"And a real-life drawbridge," added Ellie as the car whizzed across it and drew to a halt in the palace courtyard.

The palace guards snapped to attention as the Emperor and Empress of Andirovia walked majestically down the front steps. Prince John was close behind, looking uncomfortable in his naval uniform. He peered around his father and grinned at the girls.

A footman swung open the car door, and a blast of cold air rushed inside. Ellie shivered and pulled her velvet cloak tight around her shoulders. Then she climbed out and led Kate over to join the King and Queen.

"How wonderful to see you!" gushed the Empress. She kissed Ellie and Kate on the nose in the traditional Andirovian way.

"Now, come with us. We're going to inspect the palace guard."

"Oh, dear," whispered Kate. "Is that hard?"

"No," replied Ellie. "We just walk along behind Mom and Dad and get bored."

The guards looked bored, too, and very chilly. Their noses were red, their lips were blue, and some of them were struggling to keep their teeth from chattering. Ellie felt sorry for them. It couldn't be fun to have to stand out in the cold all day. She'd barely been outside for five minutes, and already she couldn't wait to get indoors.

"It's freezing," she grumbled.

"No, it's not," declared John. "It's exactly thirty-five degrees. Look—I've got this great new watch that tells the temperature as well as the time."

Ellie wasn't impressed. Cold weather might have been fun if there had been snow to play in. Without snow, she much preferred to be warm. Perhaps Andirovia wasn't such a great place for a holiday after all.

Chapter 2

The inside of the palace was even more impressive than the outside. To Ellie's relief, it was also much warmer. A flurry of maids met them in the entrance hall with mugs of hot chocolate topped with whipped cream and marshmallows. Ellie sipped hers gratefully, wrapping her hands around it to thaw out her cold fingers.

She would have loved a second helping,

but there wasn't time. The Emperor and Empress were eager to show off their home, so they whisked the visitors away for a tour. Ellie loved the log fires that blazed in every room. The light from the flickering flames glittered on the swords and shields that hung on the walls.

By the time the girls were shown to their bedrooms, the maids had already unpacked their clothes. Ellie found it reassuring to see her dressing gown hanging on the back of the door and her pink alarm clock on the bedside table. They helped her feel more at home.

She opened the small suitcase on the bed—the one she'd asked the maid not to touch. Inside were her riding clothes. She buried her face in them, breathing in the welcome smell of ponies. Then she folded them neatly on a chair, placed her riding hat on top, and went back to the suitcase.

There were five rectangular packages at the bottom. Ellie took them out one by one and carefully removed their tissue-paper wrappings. Inside each package was a framed photograph of one of her ponies—Shadow, Sundance, Moonbeam, Rainbow, and Starlight.

Ellie sighed. She already missed them so much. But at least the photos made them feel less far away. She arranged them on top of a chest of drawers, so she could see them easily when she was in bed. Then she carefully moved the photo of Shadow so that it was next to the one of Sundance—the two ponies were good friends and always stood next to each other in the field.

As Ellie stood back to admire her work, Kate bounded through the door. "My room's so fantastic!" she shrieked. "I've got a huge four-poster bed, and it's really bouncy." She paused and looked at the photographs. "Great. You've brought pictures, too. That gives me an idea."

She rushed out and soon came back clutching a framed photo of a skewbald foal.

She put it down carefully beside Ellie's picture of Starlight. "That's better. Now Angel can be with her mom, and all the ponies are together."

"Boo!"

The two girls jumped and turned around to see Prince John laughing. He'd crept up behind them when they weren't looking. He looked at the pictures and said, "Wow, Angel's really grown." He hadn't seen the foal since the day she was born—the same day Ellie gave her to Kate.

"She's really smart, too," said Kate, beaming. "She's already learned to wear a halter, and she always lifts up her feet so I can clean them when I'm grooming her."

"Can you ride her yet?" asked John.

Kate laughed. "Of course not. She's still only a baby. She won't be strong enough to carry me until she's three or four."

"But that doesn't matter," said Ellie. "Kate can ride my ponies in the meantime. And speaking of ponies—when can we see yours?"

John grinned. "How about now?"

Kate looked doubtful. "Miss Stringle said we have to get ready for the banquet soon."

"Oh, we have tons of time," said John. "Come on. Follow me."

He led them down a dark and gloomy corridor. The wood-paneled walls were covered with paintings of really old people, and there were even a few pictures of wild animals in the mountains.

At the far end was a long, curving stair-case. But just as they were about to go down, they spotted Miss Stringle at the bottom.

"Oh, no!" groaned Ellie. "I bet she's looking for us."

"Then let's make sure she doesn't find you," laughed John. "It's time I showed you *our* secret passage." Back when Prince John had visited Ellie, they'd found a secret passage leading from the palace to the nearby coastline.

John ran back down the corridor and pressed hard on one of the panels. A hidden door slowly creaked open. "Quick. In here."

The two girls ran toward him. Behind her, Ellie could hear Miss Stringle's footsteps growing louder and louder as she neared the top of the stairs. Soon, the governess would step into the corridor and see them. She would be sure to take them back to their rooms to get ready, and then there wouldn't be another chance to see John's ponies until the next day.

The secret passage was the only way to escape. But Ellie and Kate both hesitated when they reached the hidden door. The passage looked very dark and scary. Who knew what could be lurking in there?

Chapter 3

There was no more time. Ellie plucked up her courage and stepped through the secret doorway. Then she grabbed Kate's hand and pulled her friend after her. John followed swiftly, pulling the door closed behind him.

They huddled together in the darkness, hardly daring to breathe while they listened to Miss Stringle's footsteps grow closer and closer. Ellie was sure her governess would stop when she reached the hidden door. But she didn't. She marched straight by without even hesitating.

"She doesn't know we're in here," squealed Ellie, after the footsteps had started to fade.

"Where is here, anyway?" asked Kate.

"I'll show you," said John, clicking on a flashlight.

"Where did you get that from?" Kate blinked as her eyes adjusted to the light.

"I leave it in here, just in case," explained John. "A good explorer can never be sure when he'll need to use a secret passage." He loved exploring almost as much as he loved ponies.

Ellie looked around. They were in a narrow brick tunnel. "Where does it go?" she asked.

"Outside," said John. "If we go to the stable this way, there's no chance of our running into Miss Stringle again."

He led the way along the passage and down a twisting, spiral stone staircase with uneven steps. It was very steep and very narrow. Ellie was glad when she reached the bottom, where John swung open a heavy door.

As soon as she stepped outside, however, she wished she'd brought her coat with her.

It was colder than ever. She was fascinated to see her breath hang like a cloud on the still air.

Ellie stood shivering with Kate as John

closed the door behind them. The outside of the door was disguised to look like stone. It blended perfectly with the surrounding wall. No one would ever have found it unless they already knew it was there.

John led them quickly around the side of the palace toward the stable. Ellie was surprised to find that it was quite different from her own stable at home. Her royal stable was arranged around an open courtyard, so that each of her ponies had a door to the outside. John's ponies were tucked inside a cozy barn. A wide passage ran down the middle. On one side of the passage was a tack room, a feed room, and a huge pile of hay and straw. On the other was a line of four stalls, only two of which were occupied.

"This one's Toffee, and this one's

Fudge," said John, pointing to each of his chestnut ponies in turn.

Ellie stroked Toffee's face and neck. "They're both beautiful," she said, as the heat from the pony's body warmed her cold fingers.

"They're like twins," laughed Kate. "How do you tell them apart?"

"That's easy," explained John. "Toffee has a tiny white mark on her nose."

It was so small that Ellie had to look carefully before she spotted it. "I wish I could try riding her."

"I don't think we have enough time before the banquet," said Kate.

"And it's nearly dark," added John.

Ellie tried not to feel too disappointed. "It's okay," she said. "We can still play with them for a bit." She divided Toffee's mane into sections and started to twist the hairs into neat plaits.

Before she'd finished the first one, however, the barn door swung open. Miss Stringle marched in, and this time there was nowhere to hide.

"I've been looking for you everywhere," the governess said in a reproachful tone. "It's very late. You should be getting ready for the banquet." She seized the girls by the hands and led them unwillingly toward the door.

"We'll all go for a ride tomorrow," called John.

"But how?" asked Kate. "There's three of us and only two ponies."

"Darn," said Ellie. They couldn't leave one person behind—that wouldn't be fair. And riding would be more fun if they all went together. But she really wanted to ride. She hadn't been on a pony since she left home, and she couldn't bear the thought of not riding for the whole week she would be in Andirovia. There must be something they could do.

Chapter 4

Miss Stringle marched the girls to their rooms and waited impatiently while they each bathed in sweet-smelling pink bubbles and changed into their evening clothes.

Soon, Ellie was dressed in a pink silk ball gown. It had flouncy sleeves, and the skirt was embroidered with golden horseshoes. Her sandals were gold, too, and so was her tiara.

Miss Stringle inspected her carefully, straightening the hem of her dress and patting her curls into place. She was just wiping a smudge from Ellie's cheek when Kate stepped nervously into the room.

"Do I look all right?" asked Kate. "Grandma made this for me." The dress was pale blue, and the material shimmered as she moved.

"You look great!" said Ellie. She had never seen her friend look so pretty before.

But Miss Stringle seemed less sure. "It just needs a little something more." She pulled a large bunch of ribbons from her bag, selected two silver ones, and gently tied them in Kate's hair.

Kate looked at herself in the mirror and

smiled. "Thank you. They look perfect."

"You're welcome, dear," said Miss Stringle with a warm smile. Then she switched to a more matter-of-fact voice and continued, "Now, come along with me, and remember your manners. Sit up straight. Do not stick spoons on your noses. Use the correct utensil for each course. Do not slurp your soup. . . ."

The list went on and on. It lasted all the way to the banquet hall. As they followed the King and Queen through the door, Kate whispered, "I'll never remember all that."

"You'll be fine," Ellie whispered back. "Just do what I do."

The banquet hall looked beautiful. The

tables were covered with snow-white cloths and decorated with bowls of red roses and swans carved out of ice. The knives and forks were made of gold, and so were the candlesticks. Ellie loved the gentle glow of the candles, which made everything sparkle.

Ellie was pleased to find that she and Kate were sitting next to John. She was less pleased when the butler ladled soup into her china bowl. It was a strange green color and had a fishy smell. But at least it was easy to find the correct soup spoon among the wide selection of cutlery that lay before her. She picked it up very slowly and waited until she was sure Kate had followed her example. Then she pushed her sleeves out of the way, dipped her spoon in, and started to eat.

The soup tasted even worse than it looked. It had been flavored with chili powder and was spicier than any curry Ellie had ever eaten. But she didn't want to seem rude, so she made an effort to eat it all. By the time she had finished, her tongue felt as if it were on fire. Desperate to cool her mouth, she gulped down her entire glass of lemonade. Out of the corner of her eye, she noticed Kate do the same.

A maid whisked away the empty soup bowls and replaced them with gold-rimmed plates. Then the butler returned and served something small, black, and crispy.

Ellie eyed the lump of food suspiciously. There was something vaguely familiar about its shape, but she couldn't quite tell what it was. "It looks disgusting," she whispered.

"It is," said John. "But it's a dish they always serve when visitors come."

Ellie wondered whether to cut it into little pieces or just eat the whole thing all at once. Making up her mind, she stabbed it with her fork and popped the whole thing in her mouth.

Kate was more cautious. She examined the black lump on the end of her fork and asked, "What's it called?"

"Andirovian Slug Surprise," announced John.

Ellie nearly choked. She longed to spit the slug out, but she knew she couldn't. Now that it was in her mouth, she had to eat it. She summoned all her courage and forced herself to bite it in half. As soon as her teeth bit into the crisp outer shell, thick goo trickled out. It was bitter and disgusting.

Ellie swallowed as hard as she could.

The two pieces of slug slid down her throat, but they left their awful taste behind. She needed a long drink to wash it out of her mouth.

Her glass, however, was empty. She'd already drunk all the lemonade, to cool her tongue after the spicy soup. Ellie looked around the table desperately. The taste of slug was unbearable. There must be something else she could drink, she thought.

She lunged forward and grabbed the water jug. But, in her haste, she forgot about the flouncy sleeve of her ball gown, which ended up knocking over two glasses, a salt-shaker, and a bottle of vinegar. They rolled down the table and knocked down several other glasses, which, in turn, knocked down even more. The disaster spread down the long table like a row of tumbling dominoes. Stains spread across the once-white cloth, and guests leaped to their feet to avoid being spilled on.

Kate put her hand across her mouth to keep herself from giggling. "Should I still follow you?" she asked.

A small part of Ellie wanted to laugh, too. But the rest of her didn't. She'd ruined the meal, and she knew she was in big trouble. She just didn't know what sort of trouble that would be. Perhaps she'd be grounded, like the children she'd read about in her pony books. Then her entire vacation in Andirovia would be ruined. There'd be no snowballs, no exploring, and, worst of all, no riding ponies.

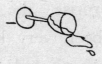

Chapter 5

Ellie found it hard to sleep that night.

To her surprise, the Emperor and Empress had been very kind about the mishap. They'd gently ordered the maids to clear up the mess, and they'd never mentioned any type of punishment. But the King and Queen had glowered at her angrily, and Miss Stringle had threatened her with extra lessons on table manners once they got home.

But there was another reason Ellie couldn't sleep. She was cold. The roaring log fire in her room had died down to a dull glow that gave out little heat. Cold drafts blew through the gaps in the windows and made her shiver. She wished she were back at home. For once, she didn't mind the fact that her bedroom was too pink. She just wanted to cuddle up under her favorite blanket—the one decorated with pictures of ponies.

At last, she decided there was no point in tossing and turning any longer. She snuggled under the heavy blankets, turned on a lamp, and started to read her book. The picture on the cover made her feel homesick—it was a palomino pony, just like Moonbeam. In the story, it belonged to two children who faced exactly the same problem as Ellie and her friends—they couldn't go out for a ride together. But they had found a solution. One person would ride a bicycle while the other was on the pony.

That could work for us, too, thought Ellie, as she finally started to fall asleep. I hope John's got a bicycle.

"Of course I have one," declared John at breakfast time. "It's the best mountain bike in Andirovia. It's red."

"Is the color important?" asked Kate.

"Even pink would do," said Ellie. She gulped down the last of her toast and leaped to her feet. "Come on," she said. Then she remembered her manners. She sat down again, folded her napkin neatly, and asked,

"May we please be excused from the table?"

"We're all going riding," explained John.

"No, you're not," said the Emperor.

"The ponies will have to wait until this afternoon," said the King. "We're being taken on an outing this morning."

"To see our new ice-cream factory," explained the Empress, smiling enthusiastically. "I'm sure you'll find it fascinating."

Ellie didn't find the outing all that fascinating. She liked ice cream. But she found it difficult to get excited about shiny pipes and big vats of glop. She didn't even enjoy the tasting session. The weather in Andirovia was so chilly that she wondered why anyone there would want to eat ice cream at all. Hot chocolate and marshmallows would have been much more appealing.

The rest of the morning dragged by slowly. The trip to the ice-cream factory was followed by a long, boring lunch with the local mayor. But eventually, the meal was over, and the children were finally free to go for their ride. Ellie and Kate were determined not to let the cold weather ruin their afternoon, so they dressed as warmly as they could. They wore thick fleeces under their outer jackets, two pairs of socks each inside their riding boots, and toasty riding gloves on their hands.

John was waiting for them outside

40

the barn with Toffee and Fudge. They were already saddled and bridled. "I asked Ivan, the groom, to get them ready," he explained. "I didn't want to waste any more time that could be spent riding."

"Who's going on the bike first?" asked Kate.

"I will," said John. "It is mine, after all."

"Can I ride Toffee, then?" asked Ellie. "She's the one I wanted to ride yesterday."

John laughed. "Only if you can tell which one she is."

Ellie inspected the two ponies carefully and soon spotted the telltale white mark on Toffee's nose. "This one," she announced, as she took the pony's reins. After checking to see that the girth was tight enough, she swung herself into the saddle. Kate followed her lead and mounted Fudge.

John proudly got his gleaming red mountain bike from the barn. "It's got twenty-four gears, alloy wheels, and a top-of-the-line computer."

"Who needs a computer on a bike?" asked Kate.

John looked at her in shock. "Why, everyone does. It tells you your current speed, your average speed, your maximum speed, how far you've gone, how many times you've turned the pedals, and . . ."

"Okay, that's enough," said Kate. "I get the picture."

"And it's got a stopwatch, so we'll know when it's time to switch," John continued, completely ignoring her interruption.

"That does sound useful," said Ellie.

"It is," said John. He leaned forward and pressed a button on the computer. "Now, let's get going."

It was wonderful to be riding again. Toffee and Fudge obviously thought so, too. They moved along willingly, with their ears pricked and their necks arched.

"Which way shall we go?" asked Ellie, as

they clattered across the drawbridge. "Can we go up to where the snow is?"

John laughed and shook his head. "It's much farther away than it looks. Let's explore the pine forest instead. The paths there will be good for the bike."

Soon they were deep in the forest, trotting among the tall trees. Ellie was enjoying herself despite her disappointment about not being able to ride in the snowy mountains. She felt warmer now that she was on the move, and she loved the smell of the crisp, cold air. It was very different from riding at home. Everything was very quiet. The ground was covered with a thick layer of pine needles, so the ponies' feet hardly made a sound.

After a while, the silence was broken by a

loud beeping. "Time to switch," called John, as he reset the computer. "It's your turn to ride the bike, Ellie."

As soon as they'd switched, Ellie discovered that John's bike was harder to ride than she'd thought. The pine needles on the path made pedaling difficult. The gears didn't help much, either. There were so many of them that she didn't know which one to use.

She was soon out of breath, but she didn't complain. Taking the bike along had been

her idea in the first place, and she was determined to keep up. Then John and Kate pushed the ponies into a canter. Ellie tried to pedal faster, but her legs were too tired. Soon Toffee and Fudge were well ahead, their hooves flying along the path as it curved around the edge of a clearing.

Ellie was about to admit defeat when she spotted a way to catch up. If she cut straight across the middle of the clearing, she would reach the other side at the same time as the ponies.

She rode off the path as fast as she could and headed for the other side. But the ground was much bumpier than it looked, and the bushes had long thorns that tore at her clothes.

"Be careful!" yelled John, looking back to

check on Ellie. But it was too late. A dead branch caught the front wheel. The bike stopped instantly, and Ellie sailed over the handlebars.

Luckily, only her pride was hurt. She clambered to her feet just as the others trotted over.

"Thank goodness you're all right," said Kate.

"What about my bike?" asked John.

Ellie pulled it upright and checked it carefully. The red paint still gleamed. The computer was still ticking away the minutes until it was time to switch again. But there was a long thorn sticking out of the front wheel. The tire was completely flat.

Chapter 6

"I'm so sorry," said Ellie, as she pulled the thorn out of the tire. The last of the air escaped with a gentle hiss.

"Can the computer fix flat tires?" teased Kate.

"Of course not," said John. "But I can. I've got the best repair kit in the country. It's got explorer-grade superglue, extra-strong patches, and an electronic gadget to measure the tire pressure." His confident smile faded as he reached into each of his pockets in turn.

Then his ears turned pink with embarrassment. "I think I've left it at home," he admitted in a quiet voice.

"It's all my fault," said Ellie. "You two go on and enjoy your ride. I'll meet you back at the stable." She picked the bike up and started to push it back the way they'd come.

"That's not fair," said Kate. "It could have happened to any of us, and it won't be much fun without you."

"Kate's right," agreed John. "And you might get lost on your way back. We'll all go home together."

They turned the ponies around and headed back to the palace. Luckily, John knew a shortcut, so they reached the stable sooner than Ellie expected.

"It's a pity it all went wrong," she said, as she pushed the bike into the barn. Then she stopped and stared in surprise. The barn wasn't empty. In the stall at the far end stood  the biggest horse she had ever seen. "Who's that?" she asked.

"His name's Goliath," answered John. "He belongs to Ivan, the groom. I'll introduce you as soon as we've tied up Toffee and Fudge."

The horse looked even bigger close up. He was jet black, with a huge head, a strong neck, and enormous hooves. But he seemed very gentle. He pricked his ears forward happily when Ellie reached up to stroke his face. Then he rubbed his head against her shoulder and nearly knocked her over.

"I don't understand," said Kate. "Why didn't we see him yesterday?"

"Because he wasn't here," John explained. "He only came back this morning. Ivan's brother had borrowed him. He loves riding, but he doesn't have a horse of his own."

"I know how he feels," said Kate. She had longed for a pony of her own for a long time before Ellie gave her Angel.

"It's a shame Goliath's not a pony," said Ellie. "If he were, we could borrow him and all go riding together."

John's eyes lit up with excitement. "Let's

do it anyway. I'm a really good rider. I'm sure I can handle him."

"I'm not so sure," said Kate, a worried expression on her face.

"Neither am I," agreed Ellie. "He's much too big for you."

"No, he's not," John insisted. He straightened his back to make himself look as tall as possible. "Anyway, that doesn't matter. Jockeys are short, and they ride big horses."

Ellie knew that that was true. But it didn't calm her fears. She suspected that even a racehorse would look small beside Goliath. He looked strong enough to carry a knight in full armor. "Maybe we should ask Ivan," she suggested.

"We can't," said John. "I don't know where he is, and we won't have enough time to ride if we go looking for him."

"But suppose he comes back before we do," said Kate. "He'll think someone has stolen Goliath."

"Not if we leave a note," replied John. He led the way to the tack room to get Goliath's saddle and bridle.

Putting the bridle on was easier than any of them expected. The gentle horse lowered his head for them to reach and opened his mouth so they could slip the metal bit between his teeth. Putting on the saddle was a much harder task. It was big and heavy, and Goliath's back was a long way up. None of them could lift the saddle high enough.

"I wish he could kneel down like a camel," said Kate. "Then we'd be able to reach."

Ellie ran to the tack room and came back carrying a battered wooden chair. "If we can't make him shorter, we'll have to make ourselves taller. Hold his head, both of you. Make sure he doesn't move."

She picked up the saddle, moved the chair as close as she could to Goliath, and climbed onto it. The extra height made all the difference. She managed to place the saddle on the horse's back. She was careful to put it slightly in front of where it should have gone. Then she slid it back into the right position to make sure all the hairs on Goliath's back were lying flat.

She fastened the girth that held

the saddle in place. Then she jumped down and carried the chair outside. "You'll need this," she told John. "You'll never get on him without it."

Kate followed her, leading Goliath, while John paused for a moment to stick a note on the stable door.

Gone for a
ride with Goliath.
Back before dark.

H.R.H
Prince John!

The huge, black horse really was a gentle giant. After having waited patiently while they struggled to put on his saddle, he now stood completely still again while John clambered up on his back from the chair. But as soon as Goliath felt his rider's weight on his back, he was eager to be on the move. He stamped his feet restlessly while John shortened the stirrups.

Kate held the horse's head to stop him from walking away. She looked at John and giggled. "You look tiny up there. Like a button on a mountain."

John ignored her comments. He shortened the reins and announced, "You can let go now. I'm in control."

Kate did as she was told and ran into the barn with Ellie to fetch the ponies. When they led them outside a few moments later, they found Goliath walking around in small circles.

"Are you all right?" asked Ellie.

"Of course I am," said John. But his voice sounded less confident than it had earlier. "He's just restless, that's all. He'll be fine once we get moving."

This time it was Ellie's turn to ride Fudge, while Kate took Toffee. John continued to ride in circles while they mounted. Then he let the big horse lead the way across the drawbridge and out to the grounds.

Goliath didn't want to walk. He kept snorting through his enormous nostrils and trying to go faster. "Steady, boy," pleaded John, struggling to keep the horse under control. He sat down firmly in the saddle and kept a tight hold on the reins.

As they left the shelter of the palace, Ellie noticed for the first time that the weather had changed. Thick clouds had blown in from the north, covering the sky with a heavy, gray blanket and hiding the tops of the mountains. A chill wind stung their cheeks and lifted the ponies' manes. It seemed to make Goliath even more restless.

"Maybe we *should* have a trot," said Ellie. "A good, long trot would use up some of his energy."

John nodded nervously. He lengthened the reins a little, and Goliath started to jog. The huge horse was very excited now. He tossed his head from side to side and snorted again. Then he dropped his head down toward his knees.

The movement happened so suddenly that John was nearly pulled over Goliath's shoulder. To save himself, he had to let the reins slip through his fingers. The enormous horse immediately noticed what had happened. Realizing his rider had lost control, Goliath raised his head again and quickly bolted away into the distance.

Chapter 7

Ellie and Kate watched in horror as Goliath galloped off across an open stretch of grass, his huge hooves thundering over the ground.

"Stop him!" yelled Kate.

"I can't," wailed John. He'd caught hold of the reins again and was pulling on them as hard as he could. But Goliath was too strong for him. He didn't want to obey his rider; he was enjoying himself too much.

"Come on, we've got to follow them," said Ellie, squeezing her legs urgently against Fudge's sides.

The chestnut pony responded immediately, starting to canter and then increasing to a gallop, racing after Goliath, with Kate and Toffee close behind.

Ellie bent low over Fudge's neck, urging the pony to go faster and faster. Normally, she loved galloping. But this time she was too scared to enjoy it. She just concentrated on following Goliath. He'd reached the end of the open grassland, and was hurtling into a wooded area. But he still didn't slow down. He raced on at full speed, twisting and turning among the trees.

The ponies rushed after him. Their manes and tails streamed behind them in the wind as they galloped on and on, farther and farther from the palace. The race seemed to be going on forever. Ellie couldn't remember the last time she had galloped that far.

But Goliath's legs were so long that he could cover the ground much faster than Toffee and Fudge could. There was no way they could keep up with the huge horse. Although Ellie and Kate urged the ponies on as much as they could, the distance between them and Goliath kept increasing.

Ellie kept her eyes on Goliath. She hoped desperately that John would stay in the saddle and not fall off. But it became harder and harder to keep the huge horse in sight as the gap between them grew. Eventually, Goliath galloped behind a clump of trees and disappeared from sight.

"Oh, no!" groaned Kate. "We've lost them."

Ellie's stomach knotted in fear, but she tried to stay calm. There was nothing to be gained by panicking now. "We'll find him. I'm sure we will," she said, as much to convince herself as to reassure her friend.

"We've got to," said Kate. "We can't leave him out here on his own."

"And we need him to show us the way back," added Ellie. They had zigzagged so much during the long gallop that she'd completely lost her sense of direction.

Toffee and Fudge were tired. They had done their best, but they were puffing hard and wanted to slow down. Ellie knew it wasn't fair to push them any harder. "We'd better let them rest," she said.

The ponies seemed happy to stop. They stood with their heads down and their sides heaving, as they struggled to get their breath back. Their necks were soaked with sweat in spite of the cold weather.

"Goliath must be tired, too," said Kate. "Maybe he'll stop soon."

"I hope so," said Ellie, turning up the collar of her coat to protect herself from the cold wind. "Let's go and look. We need to keep the ponies moving anyway, or they'll get chilled."

She pushed Fudge into a walk, letting the reins go slack so the pony could stretch her neck. Kate did the same with Toffee, and side by side they rode over to the last place they'd seen John and Goliath.

"John!" shouted Ellie. There was no reply.

"Can you hear us?" yelled Kate.

Still nothing.

"We'll have to go on a bit farther," said Ellie. She rode Fudge to the next clump of trees and called again. "John? Where are you?"

This time there was an answering shout. "I'm over here," came the faint reply.

The girls shortened their ponies' reins and trotted off in the direction of the sound.

To their delight, they soon found Goliath, with John still on his back. The huge horse had finally calmed down. He was eating grass as if nothing had happened.

John looked less happy. "That was exciting," he said, smiling weakly.

"No, that was terrifying," Kate said.

Ellie nodded in agreement. Then she giggled. "It's a good thing you didn't fall off. We'd never have gotten you back on Goliath without that chair."

John laughed. "That's why I didn't get off while I was waiting for you."

"Should we get going?" said Kate. "It's going to be a long ride back."

Ellie glanced at John. "Which way do we go?" she asked.

There was a long pause as John looked

around thoughtfully. Then he shrugged his shoulders and meekly admitted, "I don't know where we are. I think we might be lost."

Chapter 8

Ellie stared at John in disbelief. "You must know where we are. You live here!"

"Our palace grounds are much larger than yours," declared John, in his most superior voice. "I haven't gotten around to exploring all of it yet."

"Come on, don't you see anything that you recognize?" asked Kate. "How about that funny tree over there? The one that's bent over like an old man with a walking stick."

John shook his head. "I've never seen it before. Anyway, using trees as landmarks isn't a good way of finding out where you are. Real explorers use the sun and the stars and the mountaintops to guide them."

"Okay, then," said Ellie. "Let's see you do it. You're always saying how you want to be an explorer."

They all looked up at the sky. The clouds seemed even darker than they had earlier. They were lower, too. They didn't just hide the peaks of the mountains. Now they reached halfway down the slopes.

"So much for that idea," said Kate. "No

sun, no stars, and no mountaintops. What does a real explorer do at a time like this?"

John thought for a moment. Then he grinned triumphantly. "It's simple. We just follow our tracks back the way we came. I've got this great survival guide at home. It's got everything there is to know about tracking."

He pulled Goliath's head up, shortened the reins, and walked him around in a circle. As he rode, John stared intently at the ground. Then he smiled and pointed to a large hoofprint. "See that? That means Goliath and I must have come that way."

Ellie was impressed. The hoofprint was quite faint. She would never have spotted it.

"Here's another one," called John. "And there's a freshly snapped twig. Goliath must have stepped on it."

Kate and Ellie joined in the search. It was fun—like a treasure hunt. Each new sign was a fresh clue showing them the way back to the palace. Their progress was slow, because they had to look so carefully. But they were sure they would make it back eventually.

Just then, a tiny white speck floated down from the sky and landed on Fudge's mane. It lay there for a moment. Then it melted and disappeared. Soon another one fell, and then another. Ellie felt an excited thrill as she realized what they were. "It's snowing!" she cried. She looked up at the sky, letting the tiny flakes fall on her face.

"Cool!" yelled Kate. "I love snow." She

poked her tongue out and
tried to catch the flakes.

John and Ellie did the
same. Soon, all three of them
were so absorbed in their
new game that they completely
forgot about their hunt for the tracks. More
and more flakes were falling from the sky, and
they were getting bigger, too. They weren't
melting anymore when they landed. Instead,
they stayed on the ground, covering it with a
carpet of white.

Ellie rode up to a tree and ran her hand
along a branch, picking up the snow that had
settled there. "I've got a snowball," she sang,
holding it above her head as if she were
about to throw it at John.

"Don't!" he pleaded. "If you hit Goliath,

he might run off again."

Ellie grinned. "I was only teasing." She threw the ball at the tree instead. It hit the trunk with a satisfying thud and smashed to pieces. She'd started a new game. Soon, they were all making snowballs and tossing them at the trees.

Kate was the first to get tired. "I'm getting hungry," she said. "Let's go back."

Ellie looked around. The world looked completely different now. Everything was covered with a smooth blanket of pure, white snow. It hid the ground, the grass, and the fallen twigs.

To her horror, Ellie realized it also hid all the tracks they had been following.

It was impossible to find them now. And without those tracks, they wouldn't be able to find their way home.

Chapter 9

Ellie bit her lip nervously. "What do we do now?"

"Panic?" suggested Kate, only half joking.

"Don't be silly," said John. "Explorers never panic." He pointed a way through the falling snow. "I'm pretty sure we came from over there."

Ellie nodded. Far off in the distance, she could faintly see the strange shape of the tree

Kate had pointed out earlier. "Does that help?" she asked, gesturing toward the tree.

"It sure does," said John. "If we know where we were before, and we know where we are now, we can work out the direction we've been traveling in. So, if we keep going the same way, we'll get home."

"I hope so," said Kate, shivering. "My gloves are wet from making snowballs, and my fingers are cold."

"Mine, too," agreed Ellie. She wasn't completely sure she understood John's plan, but she was willing to give it a try. "Let's get moving. It's freezing."

"You're right," said John, checking the thermometer on his watch. "It's now exactly thirty-two degrees. Freezing." Then he shortened his reins and announced, "I'll go in front. I'm the most experienced at exploring." He made Goliath walk forward and set off slowly, looking back occasionally to make sure the others were still following.

Ellie let Kate and Toffee go next; she and Fudge went last. The snow didn't seem as exciting now. There was already so much of it, and it was still falling steadily.

As they rode on, the weather got even worse. The snow fell faster and faster. The wind grew stronger, too, whipping the flakes into their faces and stinging their cheeks. They rode hunched up against the cold, their heads turned down to gain some protection from the brims of their hats.

Soon they were riding through a world of whirling white. Ellie glanced back to see if they were still traveling in a straight line. But the falling flakes covered their hoofprints so quickly that it wasn't possible to tell anymore. "Are you sure we're going the right way?" she shouted.

"Of course I am," John called back. "Trust me. I know what I'm doing."

It was snowing even harder now. The flakes fell so close together that it was hard to see. Ellie felt as though she were surrounded by a white wall. She urged Fudge to walk faster to keep close to the others. She didn't want to get separated from them in this blizzard.

At first, the pony seemed happy to obey. She trudged through the snow, following Toffee without Ellie's having to do much to guide her. But then she started to act strangely. First she tried to turn to the right. Then she tried to turn to the left. Then she tried to whirl around and go the other way.

"Please, stop it," begged Ellie. The ride was turning into a battle of wills between her and the chestnut pony. She was determined to win. It was bad enough being lost with John and Kate. It would be dreadful to be out there in the snow on her own.

She tightened the reins and kept her legs close to Fudge's sides. Every time the pony started to dart away, Ellie managed to stop her. But it was hard work. Soon she was sweating inside her jacket despite the cold weather.

Kate turned around and saw what was going on. "What's wrong?" she asked.

"She won't do as she's told," wailed Ellie. "She doesn't want to follow you. She wants to go off on her own."

"That's weird," called John from the front. "She's usually very well behaved."

"Maybe it's the weather," suggested Kate. "It's a bit scary when you can't see anything except snow!"

Ellie figured Kate was probably right. It sounded like a good explanation.

Soon the snow started to lighten up. With fewer flakes falling, they could see farther through the white wilderness that surrounded them. But Fudge continued to act strangely.

Something else must be wrong, thought Ellie.

"Look," said Kate. "There's another one of those strange-shaped trees."

Ellie stared at it. It looked exactly like an old man with a walking stick. "That's weird," she said. "You wouldn't expect to have two trees like that so close together."

Then she had a dreadful thought.

"You don't think . . . ?" Her voice died away. She didn't want to say it out loud.

But John did it for her. "It's the same tree," he sighed. "We've gone around in a circle."

Chapter 10

Goliath and Toffee stood beside the tree quietly with their heads down. They looked as tired and miserable as their riders felt. Snow covered their manes and frosted their ears. But Fudge was still restless. She kept stamping her feet and trying to walk away.

Ellie felt a rising tide of panic as she struggled to make the pony stand still. They really were completely lost. "What are we going to do?" she asked, feeling a little hopeless.

"I'm not sure yet," replied John. "There's no point in following our tracks again. They'll only bring us back here."

"We can't see them anyway," said Kate. "The snow's already covered them up." She looked around nervously and added, "It'll start getting dark soon."

Ellie shivered, partly from cold and partly from fear. "We'll freeze if we're out here all night."

"No, we won't," said John. "We can build an igloo. I've read all about how to do it in my survival guide.  You just take big chunks of snow and . . ."

"Stop!" yelled Kate. "I don't want to do

that. I just want to go home."

"So do I," said Ellie. "There might be wild animals out here." She recalled the scary pictures she'd seen in the secret passageway back at the palace.

"There aren't that many," said John brightly. "Just the Andirovian silver-backed wolf, and that's an endangered species."

This was more than Kate could handle. "I'm scared!" she cried. "I'm tired, and I'm cold, and I'm very, very hungry."

"I think the ponies are, too," said Ellie, suddenly aware of her own empty stomach.

"Maybe that's what's wrong with Fudge," suggested John. "She eats a lot more than Toffee does. When I take her out on a ride, she's always in a hurry to get back for her feeding."

His words gave Ellie a glimmer of hope. "Do you mean she's one of those ponies that always seems to know when you've turned toward home?"

"Definitely," said John. "She always speeds up when we're heading back."

A slow smile spread across Ellie's face. "If she's trying to go home now, that might mean she knows the way."

"Or it might not," Kate said gloomily.

"But it's worth a try," said Ellie. "We've got nothing to lose."

"And we can always build an igloo later," added John.

Ellie let the reins slip through her fingers until they hung so loosely that Fudge was free to go in whichever direction she pleased. Then Ellie squeezed her legs against the pony's sides. "Go on, girl. Take us home."

Fudge didn't need any more encouragement. She turned and walked away from the strange-looking tree in a very determined fashion. Toffee and Goliath followed her, their hooves crunching on the snow.

Sometimes, Fudge led them between trees whose branches sagged under the weight of the fallen snow. Sometimes, she plunged through snowdrifts that reached her knees. But she never hesitated. She really seemed to know where she was going.

At long last, they rode out from a patch of pine trees and saw the palace straight ahead of them in the distance. Fudge whinnied in triumph and seemed to find a new store of energy. She started to trot, then broke into a canter. Goliath and Toffee did the same. Soon, they were all racing toward the safety of home.

Now that the end was in sight, Ellie was beginning to enjoy the ride again. She glanced at John and Kate and saw that they were smiling, too.

They slowed down as they reached the moat, trotted sedately over the drawbridge, and came to a halt in the courtyard.

As they swung themselves wearily out of their saddles, two footmen unfurled a long red carpet down the snow-covered steps. The Emperor and Empress raced down the stairs, followed closely by the King and Queen.

"We've been so worried about you," wailed the Empress. She hugged John dramatically, pulling his face so close to her chest that he looked as if he could hardly breathe.

"We were about to send out a search party," said the Queen, dabbing her eyes with a lace-trimmed handkerchief.

The Emperor looked at John sternly. "Ivan was worried that you might have had problems with Goliath."

"Oh, no," replied John, as he struggled

free of his mother's embrace. "We've had a lovely time."

Ellie knew that that wasn't a lie, but she knew it wasn't the whole truth, either. John obviously didn't want to admit what had really happened, but it looked as though he might have to if they kept questioning him. Somehow, she had to change the subject.

"Fudge was the real hero," she cried, throwing her arms around the chestnut pony's neck. "She brought us safely back."

Her plan worked. The adults were so curious to learn more about Fudge's cleverness that they didn't ask any more awkward questions about Goliath.

"You'd better come inside and get warm," said the Emperor, when the explanations were over. "Ivan can look after the horses."

"But we'll help," said John. "All real explorers look after their ponies before they look after themselves."

They led Toffee, Fudge, and Goliath back to the barn. Ivan had already put a thick layer of clean straw on the floor of each stall and hung up nets bulging with sweet-smelling hay.

Just as they finished taking off the saddles and bridles, a maid arrived carrying three large mugs of hot chocolate on a golden tray. Ellie sipped hers happily, enjoying the warm feeling she got inside. "I think I've had enough snow for today," she said.

"And enough exploring," said Kate.

"Maybe tomorrow we should stay closer to home," suggested John. Then he grinned and added, "We could build that igloo."

"Building snowmen would be more fun," said Kate.

"I've got an even better idea," said Ellie. "Let's make snow *ponies*. I bet Fudge could help with that, too."

The three children all laughed as they returned to the palace and settled in after their snowy adventure.